SPARKS OF TEMPTATION

NEW YORK TIMES BESTSELLING AUTHOR

BRENDA JACKSON

SPARKS OF TEMPTATION

A Westmoreland Novel

HARLEQUIN® KIMANI ARABESQUE®

Sparks of Temptation

ISBN-13: 978-0-373-09170-6

This edition published February 2015.

Copyright © 2015 by Harlequin Books S.A.

Recycling programs for this product may not exist in your area.

The publisher acknowledges the copyright holder of the individual works as follows:

The Proposal
Copyright © 2011 by Brenda Streater Jackson

Feeling the Heat
Copyright © 2012 by Brenda Streater Jackson

Printed in U.S.A.

CONTENTS

THE WESTMORELAND FAMILY

Scott and Delane Westmoreland

John (Evelyn) · ② ③ ④ ⑤ · **James (Sarah)** · ⑦ ① · **Corey (Abbie)** Madison

Dare (Shelly) AJ, Allison	**Thorn** (Tara) Trace	**Stone** (Madison) Rock, Regan	**Storm** (Jayla) Shanna, Johanna, Slate	**Chase** (Jessica) Carlton Scott	**Delaney** (Jamal) Ari, Arielle

⑥ ⑪ ⑧ ⑨ ⑭ ⑮

Jared (Dana) Jaren	**Spencer** (Chardonnay) Russell	**Durango** (Savannah) Sarah	**Ian** (Brooke) Pierce, Price	**Quade** (Cheyenne) Venus, Athena, Troy	**Reggie** (Olivia) Ryder

⑫ ⑬ ⑩

Clint (Alyssa) Cain	**Cole** (Patrina) Emilie, Emery	**Casey** (McKinnon) Corey Martin

① Delaney's Desert Sheikh
② A Little Dare
③ Thorn's Challenge
④ Stone Cold Surrender
⑤ Riding the Storm
⑥ Jared's Counterfeit Fiancée

⑦ The Chase is On
⑧ The Durango Affair
⑨ Ian's Ultimate Gamble
⑩ Seduction, Westmoreland Style
⑪ Spencer's Forbidden Passion
⑫ Taming Clint Westmoreland

⑬ Cole's Red-Hot Pursuit
⑭ Quade's Babies
⑮ Tall, Dark...Westmoreland!
⑯ Dreams of Forever

THE DENVER WESTMORELAND FAMILY TREE

Raphel and Gemma Westmoreland

Stern Westmoreland (Paula Bailey)

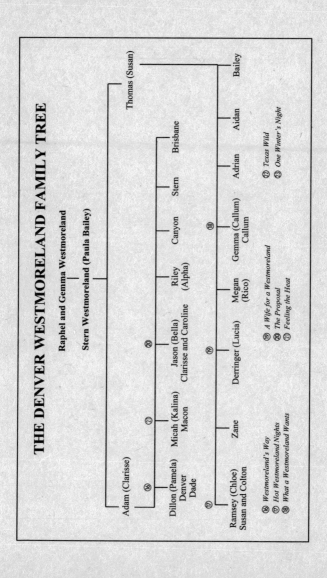

Adam (Clarisse)   Thomas (Susan)

Dillon (Pamela) ⑯   Micah (Kalina) ⑰   Jason (Bella) ⑳
Denver   Macon   Clarisse and Caroline
Dade

Riley (Alpha)   Canyon   Stern   Brisbane

Ramsey (Chloe) ⑰   Zane   Derringer (Lucia) ⑲   Megan (Rico)   Gemma (Callum) ⑱   Adrian   Aidan   Bailey
Susan and Colton   Callum

⑯ Westmoreland's Way
⑰ Hot Westmoreland Nights
⑱ What a Westmoreland Wants

⑲ A Wife for a Westmoreland
⑳ The Proposal
㉑ Feeling the Heat

㉒ Texas Wild
㉓ One Winter's Night

Dear Reader,

When I first introduced the Westmoreland family, little did I know they would become hugely popular with readers. Originally, the Westmoreland family series was intended to be just six books, Delaney and her five brothers—Dare, Thorn, Stone, Storm and Chase. Later, I wanted my readers to meet their cousins—Jared, Spencer, Durango, Ian, Quade and Reggie. Finally, there were Uncle Corey's triplets—Clint, Cole and Casey.

What began as a six-book series blossomed into a thirty-book series when I included the Denver Westmorelands. I was very happy when Harlequin Kimani Arabesque responded to my readers' requests that the earlier books be reprinted. And I'm even happier that the reissues are in a great two-in-one format.

Sparks of Temptation contains *The Proposal* and *Feeling the Heat*. These are two Westmoreland classics and are books number twenty and twenty-one in the Westmoreland series. In *The Proposal*, Jason meets Bella Bostwick and awakens to passion the likes of which he's never had before. It doesn't take long for him to figure out that Bella is the one woman whose heart he needs to conquer. And in *Feeling the Heat*, Micah intends to prove that when a Westmoreland wants something—or someone—he will stop at nothing to get it, and Micah Westmoreland wants Kalina Daniels back in his life. Grab a cold drink. It's going to be hot!

I hope you enjoy reading these special stories as much as I enjoyed writing them.

Happy reading!

Brenda Jackson

To Gerald Jackson, Sr. My one and only.

To all my readers who enjoy reading about the Westmorelands, this book is especially for you!

To my Heavenly Father. How Great Thou Art.

He hath made everything beautiful in his time.
—*Ecclesiastes* 3:11

THE PROPOSAL

Prologue

"Hello, ma'am, I'm Jason Westmoreland and I'd like to welcome you to Denver."

Even before she turned around, the deep, male voice had Bella Bostwick's stomach clenching as the throaty sound vibrated across her skin. And then when she gazed up into his eyes she had to practically force oxygen into her lungs. He had to be the most gorgeous man she'd ever seen.

For a moment she couldn't speak nor was she able to control her gaze from roaming over him and appreciating everything she saw. He was tall, way over six feet, with dark brown eyes, sculpted cheekbones and a chiseled jaw. And then there was his skin, a deep, rich chocolate-brown that had her remembering her craving for that particular treat and how delicious it was. But nothing could be more appealing than his lips and the way they were shaped. Sensuous. Sumptuous. A perfect pair for the sexy smile curving them.

He said he was a Westmoreland and because this charity ball was given on behalf of the Westmoreland Foundation, she could only assume he was one of *those* Westmorelands.

She took the hand he'd extended and wished she hadn't when a heated sizzle rode up her spine the moment she touched it. She tried forcing the sensation away. "And I'm Elizabeth Bostwick, but I prefer just Bella."

The smile curving his lips widened a fraction, enough to send warm blood rushing through her veins. "Hi, Bella."

The way he pronounced her name was ultrasexy. She thought his smile was intoxicating and definitely contagious, which was the reason she could so easily return it. "Hi, Jason."

"First, I'd like to offer my condolences on the loss of your grandfather."

"Thank you."

"And then I'm hoping the two of us could talk about the ranch you inherited. If you decide to sell it, I'd like to put in my bid for both the ranch and Hercules."

Bella drew in a deep breath. Her grandfather Herman Bostwick had died last month and left his land and prized stallion to her. She had seen the horse when she'd come to town for the reading of the will and would admit he was beautiful. She had returned to Denver from Savannah only yesterday to handle more legal matters regarding her grandfather's estate. "I haven't decided what I plan on doing regarding the ranch or the livestock, but if I do decide to sell I will keep your interest in mind. But I need to make you aware that according to my uncle Kenneth there are others who've expressed the same interest."

"Yes, I'm sure there are."

He had barely finished his sentence when her uncle suddenly appeared at her side and spoke up. "Westmoreland."

"Mr. Bostwick."

Bella immediately picked up strong negative undercurrents radiating between the two men and the extent of it became rather obvious when her uncle said in a curt tone, "It's time to leave, Bella."

She blinked. "Leave? But we just got here, Uncle Kenneth."

Her uncle smiled down at her as he tucked her arm underneath his. "Yes, dear, but you just arrived in town yesterday and have been quite busy since you've gotten here taking care of business matters."

She arched a brow as she stared at the great-uncle she only discovered she had a few weeks ago. He hadn't been concerned with how exhausted she was when he'd insisted she accompany him here tonight, saying it was her place to attend this gala in her grandfather's stead.

"Good night, Westmoreland. I'm taking my niece home."

She barely had time to bid Jason farewell when her uncle escorted her to the door. As they proceeded toward the exit she couldn't help glancing over her shoulder to meet Jason's gaze. It was intense and she could tell he hadn't appreciated her uncle's abruptness. And then she saw a smile touch his lips again and she couldn't help reciprocate by smiling back. Was he flirting with her? Was she with him?

"Jason Westmoreland is someone you don't want to get to know, Bella," Kenneth Bostwick said in a gruff tone, apparently noticing the flirtatious exchange between them.

She turned to glance up at her uncle as they walked out into the night. People were still arriving. "Why?"

"He wants Herman's land. None of the Westmorelands are worth knowing. They think they can do whatever the hell they please around these parts." He interrupted her thoughts by saying, "There're a bunch of them and they own a lot of land on the outskirts of town."

She lifted an arched brow. "Near where my grandfather lived?"

"Yes. In fact, Jason Westmoreland's land is adjacent to Herman's."

"Really?" She smiled warmly at the thought that Jason Westmoreland lived on property that connected to the land she'd inherited. Technically that made her his neighbor. *No wonder he wants to buy my land,* she thought to herself.

"It's a good thing you're selling Herman's land, but I wouldn't sell it to him under any circumstances."

She frowned when he opened the car for her to get in. "I haven't decided what I plan to do with the ranch, Uncle Kenneth," she reminded him.

He chuckled. "What is there to decide? You know nothing about ranching and a woman of your delicacy, breeding and refinement belongs back in Savannah and not here in Denver trying to run a hundred-acre ranch and enduring harsh winters. Like I told you earlier, I already know someone who wants to buy the ranch along with all the livestock—especially that stallion

Hercules. They're offering a lot of money. Just think of all the shoes, dresses and hats you'll be able to buy, not to mention a real nice place near the Atlantic Ocean."

Bella didn't say anything. She figured this was probably not the time to tell him that as far as she was concerned there was a lot to decide because none of those things he'd mentioned meant anything to her. She refused to make a decision about her inheritance too hastily.

As her uncle's car pulled out of the parking lot, she settled back against the plush leather seats and remembered the exact moment her and Jason Westmoreland's eyes had met.

It was a connection she doubted she would ever forget.

Chapter 1

One month later

"**D**id you hear Herman Bostwick's granddaughter is back in Denver and rumor has it she's here to stay?"

Jason Westmoreland's ears perked up on the conversation between his sister-in-law Pam and his two cousins-in-law Chloe and Lucia. He was at his brother Dillon's house, stretched out on the living room floor playing around with his six-month-old nephew, Denver.

Although the ladies had retired to the dining room to sit at the table and chat, it wasn't hard to hear what they were saying and he thought there was no reason for him not to listen. Especially when the woman they were discussing was a woman who'd captured his attention the moment he'd met her last month at a charity ball. She was a woman he hadn't been able to stop thinking about since.

"Her name is Elizabeth but she goes by Bella," Lucia, who'd recently married his cousin Derringer, was saying. "She came into Dad's paint store the other day and I swear she is simply beautiful. She looks so out of place here in Denver, a real Southern belle amidst a bunch of roughnecks."

"And I hear she intends to run the ranch alone. Her uncle Kenneth has made it known he won't be lifting one finger to help her," Pam said in disgust. "The nerve of the man to be so darn selfish. He was counting on her selling that land to Myers Smith who promised to pay him a bunch of money if the deal went through. It seems everyone would love to get their hands on that land and especially that stallion Hercules."

Including me, Jason thought, as he rolled the ball toward his nephew but kept his ears wide-open. He hadn't known Bella Bostwick had returned to Denver and wondered if she remembered he was interested in purchasing her land and Hercules. He definitely hoped so. His thoughts then shifted to Kenneth Bostwick. The man's attitude didn't surprise him. He'd always acted as if he was entitled, which is probably the reason Kenneth and Herman never got along. And since Herman's death, Kenneth had let it be known around town that he felt the land Bella had inherited should be his. Evidently Herman hadn't seen it that way and had left everything in his will to the granddaughter he'd never met.

"Well, I hope she's cautious as to who she hires to help out on that ranch. I can see a woman that beautiful drawing men in droves, and some will be men who she needs to be leery of," Chloe said.

Jason frowned at the thought of any man drawn to her and didn't fully understand why he reacted that way. Lucia was right in saying Bella was beautiful. He had been totally captivated the moment he'd first seen her. And it had been obvious Kenneth Bostwick hadn't wanted him anywhere near his niece.

Kenneth never liked him and had envied Jason's relationship with old man Herman Bostwick. Most people around these parts had considered Herman mean, ornery and craggy, but Jason was not one of them. He would never forget the one time he had run away from home at eleven and spent the night hidden in Bostwick's barn. The old man had found him the next morning and returned him to his parents. But not before feeding him a tasty breakfast and getting him to help gather eggs from the chickens and milk the cows. It was during that time he'd discovered Herman Bostwick wasn't as mean as everyone thought. In fact, Herman had only been a lonely old man.

Jason had gone back to visit Herman often over the years and had been there the night Hercules had been born. He'd known the moment he'd seen the colt that he would be special. And Herman had even told him that the horse would one day be his. Herman had died in his sleep a few months ago and now his ranch and every single thing on it, including Hercules, belonged to his granddaughter. Everyone assumed she would sell the ranch, but from what he was hearing she had moved to Denver from Savannah.

He hoped to hell she had thought through her decision. Colorado's winters were rough, especially in Denver. And running a spread as big as the one she'd inherited wasn't easy for an experienced rancher; he didn't want to think how it would be for someone who knew nothing about it. Granted, if she kept Marvin Allen on as the foreman things might not be so bad, but still, there were a number of ranch hands and some men didn't take kindly to a woman who lacked experience being their boss.

"I think the neighborly thing for us to do is to pay her a visit and welcome her to the area. We can also let her know if there's anything she needs she can call on us," Pam said, interrupting his thoughts.

"I agree," both Lucia and Chloe chimed in.

He couldn't help but agree, as well. Paying his new neighbor a visit and welcoming her to the area was the right thing to do, and he intended to do just that. He might have lost out on a chance to get the ranch but he still wanted Hercules.

But even more than that, he wanted to get to know Bella Bostwick better.

Bella stepped out of the house and onto the porch and looked around at the vast mountains looming before her. The picturesque view almost took her breath away and reminded her of why she had defied her family and moved here from Savannah two weeks ago.

Her overprotective parents had tried talking her out of what they saw as a foolish move on her part mainly because they hadn't wanted her out of their sight. It had been bad enough while growing up when she'd been driven to private schools by a chauffeur each day and trailed everywhere she went by a bodyguard until she was twenty-one.

And the sad thing was that she hadn't known about her grandfather's existence until she was notified of the reading of his will. She hadn't been informed in time to attend the funeral services and a part of her was still upset with her parents for keeping that from her.

She didn't know what happened to put a permanent wedge between father and son, but whatever feud that existed between them should not have included her. She'd had every right to get to know Herman Bostwick and now he was gone. When she thought about the summers she could have spent here visiting him instead of being shipped away to some camp for the summer she couldn't help but feel angry. She used to hate those camps and the snooty kids that usually went to them.

Before leaving Savannah she had reminded her parents that she was twenty-five and old enough to make her own decisions about what she wanted to do with her life. And as far as she was concerned, the trust fund her maternal grandparents had established for her, as well as this ranch she'd now inherited from her paternal grandfather, made living that life a lot easier. It was the first time in her life that she had anything that was truly hers.

It would be too much to ask David and Melissa Bostwick to see things that way and they'd made it perfectly clear that they didn't. She wouldn't be surprised if they were meeting with their attorney at this very moment to come up with a way to force her to return home to Savannah. Well, she had news for them. This was now her home and she intended to stay.

If they'd had anything to say about it she would be in Savannah and getting engaged to marry Hugh Pierce. Most women would consider Hugh, with his tall, dark and handsome looks and his old-money wealth, a prime catch. And if she really thought hard about it, then she would be one of those women who thought so. But that was the problem. She had to think real hard about it. They'd dated a number of times but there was never any connection, any spark and no real enthusiasm on her part about spending time with him. She had tried as delicately as she could to explain such a thing to her parents but that hadn't stopped them from trying to shove Hugh down her throat every chance they got. That only proved how controlling they could be.

And speaking of controlling...her uncle Kenneth had become another problem. He was her grandfather's fifty-year-old half brother, whom she'd met for the first time when she'd flown in for the reading of the will. He'd assumed the ranch would go to him and had been gravely disappointed that day to discover it hadn't. He had also expected her to sell everything, and when she'd made the decision to keep the ranch, he had been furious and said his kindness to her had ended, and that he wouldn't lift a finger to help and wanted her to find out the hard way just what a mistake she had made.

She sank into the porch swing, thinking there was no way she could have made a mistake in deciding to build a life here. She had fallen in love with the land the first time she'd seen it when she'd come for the reading of the will. And it hadn't taken long to decide even though she'd been robbed of the opportunity to connect with her grandfather in life, she would connect with him in death by accepting the gift he'd given her. A part of her felt that although they'd never met, he had somehow known about the miserable childhood she had endured and was giving her the chance to have a way better adult life.

The extra men she had hired to work the ranch so

far seemed eager to do so and appreciated the salary she was paying them which, from what she'd heard, was more than fair. She'd always heard if you wanted good people to work for you then you needed to pay them good money.

She was about to get up to go back into the house to pack up more of her grandfather's belongings when she noticed someone on horseback approaching in the distance. She squinted her eyes, remembering this was Denver and people living on the outskirts of town, in the rural sections, often traveled by horseback, and she was grateful for the riding lessons her parents had insisted that she take. She'd always wanted to own a horse and now she had several of them.

As the rider came closer she felt a tingling sensation in the pit of her stomach when she recognized him. Jason Westmoreland. She definitely remembered him from the night of the charity ball, and one of the things she remembered the most was his warm smile. She had often wondered if he'd been as ruggedly handsome as she recalled. The closer the rider got she realized he was.

And she had to admit that in the three times she'd been to Denver, he was the closest thing to a modern-day cowboy she had seen. Even now he was riding his horse with an expertise and masculinity that had her heart pounding with every step the horse took. His gaze was steady on her and she couldn't help but stare back. Heat crawled up her spine and waves of sensuous sensations swept through her system. She could feel goose bumps form on her skin. He was definitely the first and only man she'd ever been this attracted to.

She couldn't help wondering why he was paying her

a visit. He had expressed interest in her land and in Hercules when she'd met him that night at the charity ball. Was he here to convince her she'd made a mistake in moving here like her parents and uncle had done? Would he try to talk her into selling the land and horse to him? If that was the case then she had the same news for him she'd had for the others. She was staying put and Hercules would remain hers until she decided otherwise.

He brought his horse to a stop at the foot of the porch near a hitching post. "Hello, Bella."

"Jason." She gazed up into the dark brown eyes staring at her and could swear she felt heat radiating from them. The texture of his voice tingled against her skin just as it had that night. "Is there a reason for your visit?"

A smile curved his lips. "I understand you've decided to try your hand at ranching."

She lifted her chin, knowing what was coming next. "That's right. Do you have a problem with it?"

"No, I don't have a problem with it," he said smoothly. "The decision was yours to make. However, I'm sure you know things won't be easy for you."

"Yes, I'm very much aware they won't be. Is there anything else you'd like to say?"

"Yes. We're neighbors and if you ever need my help in any way just let me know."

She blinked. Had he actually offered his help? There had to be a catch and quickly figured what it was. "Is the reason you're being nice that you still want to buy Hercules? If so, you might as well know I haven't made a decision about him yet."

His smile faded and the look on his face suddenly

became intense. "The reason I'm being *nice* is that I think of myself as a nice person. And as far as Hercules is concerned, yes, I still want to buy him, but that has nothing to do with my offering my help to you as your neighbor."

She knew she had offended him and immediately regretted it. She normally wasn't this mistrusting of people, but owning the ranch was a touchy subject with her because so many people were against it. He had wanted the land and Hercules but had accepted her decision and was even offering his help when her own uncle hadn't. Instead of taking it at face value, she'd questioned it. "Maybe I shouldn't have jumped to conclusions."

"Yes, maybe you shouldn't have."

Every cell in her body started to quiver under the intensity of his gaze. At that moment she knew his offer had been sincere. She wasn't sure how she knew; she just did. "I stand corrected. I apologize," she said.

"Apology accepted."

"Thank you." And because she wanted to get back on good footing with him she asked, "How have you been, Jason?"

His features relaxed when he said, "Can't complain." He tilted his Stetson back from his eyes before dismounting from the huge horse as if it was the easiest of things to do.

And neither can I complain, she thought, watching him come up the steps of the porch. There was nothing about seeing him in all his masculine form that any woman could or would complain about. She felt her throat tighten when moments later he was standing in front of her. Something she could recognize as hot, fluid desire closed in on her, making it hard to breathe. Especially when his gaze was holding hers with the same concentration he'd had the night of the ball.

Today in the bright sunlight she was seeing things about him that the lights in the ballroom that night hadn't revealed: the whiteness of his teeth against his dark skin, the thickness of his lashes, the smooth texture of his skin and the broadness of his shoulders beneath his shirt. Another thing she was seeing now as well as what she remembered seeing in full detail that night was the full shape of a pair of sensual lips.

"And what about you, Bella?"

She blinked, realizing he'd spoken. "What about me?" The smile curving his lips returned and in a way that lulled her into thoughts she shouldn't be thinking, like how she'd love kissing that smile on his face.

"How have you been…besides busy?" he asked.

Bella drew in a deep breath and said, "Yes, things have definitely been busy and at times even crazy."

"I bet. And I meant what I said earlier. If you ever need help with anything, let me know."

"Thanks for the offer, I appreciate it." She had seen the turnoff to his ranch. The marker referred to it as Jason's Place. And from what she'd seen through the trees it was a huge ranch and the two-story house was beautiful.

She quickly remembered her manners and said, "I was about to have a cup of tea. Would you like a cup, as well?"

He leaned against the post and his smile widened even more. "Tea?"

"Yes."

She figured he found such a thing amusing if the smile curving his lips was anything to go by. The last thing a cowboy would want after being in the saddle was a cup of tea. A cold beer was probably more to his liking but was the one thing she didn't have in her refrigerator. "I'd understand if you'd rather not," she said.

He chuckled. "A cup of tea is fine."

"You sure?"

He chuckled again. "Yes, I'm positive."

"All right then." She opened the door and he followed her inside.

Besides the fact Jason thought she looked downright beautiful, Bella Bostwick smelled good, as well. He wished there was some way he could ignore the sudden warmth that flowed through his body from her scent streaming through his nostrils.

And then there was the way she was dressed. He had to admit that although she looked downright delectable in her jeans and silk blouse she also looked out of place in them. But as she walked gracefully in front of him, Jason thought that a man could endure a lot of sleepless nights dreaming about a Southern-belle backside shaped like hers.

"If you'll have a seat, Jason, I'll bring the tea right out."

He stopped walking as he realized she must have a pot already made. "All right."

He watched her walk into the kitchen, but instead of taking the seat like she'd offered, he kept standing as he glanced around taking in the changes she'd already made to the place. There were a lot of framed art pieces on the wall, a number of vases filled with flowers, throw rugs on the wood floor and fancy curtains attached to the windows. It was evident that a woman lived here. And she was some woman.

She hadn't hesitated to get her back up when she'd assumed his visit here was less than what he'd told her. He figured Kenneth Bostwick, in addition to no telling how many others, probably hadn't liked her decision not to sell her land and was giving her pure grief about it. He wouldn't be one of those against her decision.

He continued to glance around the room, noting the changes. There were a lot of things that remained the same, like Herman's favorite recliner, but she'd added a spiffy new sofa to go with it. It was just as well. The old one had seen better days. The old man had claimed he would be getting a new one this coming Christmas, not knowing when he'd said it he wouldn't be around.

Jason drew in a deep breath remembering the last time he'd seen Herman Bostwick alive. It had been a month before he'd died. Jason had come to check on him and to ride Hercules. Jason was one of the few people who could do so mainly because he was the one Herman had let break in the horse.

He glanced down to study the patterns on the throw rug beneath his feet, thinking how unique looking they were when he heard her reenter the room. He looked up and a part of him wished he hadn't. The short, medium-brown curls framing her face made her mahogany-colored skin appear soft to the touch and perfect for her hazel eyes and high cheekbones.

There was a refinement about her, but he had a feeling she was a force to be reckoned with if she had to be. She'd proven that earlier when she'd assumed he was there to question her sanity about moving here. Maybe he should be questioning his own sanity for not convincing her to move on and return to where she came from. No matter her best intentions, she wasn't cut out to be a rancher, not with her soft hands and manicured nails.

He believed there had to be some inner conflict driving her to try to run the ranch. He decided then and there that he would do whatever he could to help her succeed. And as she set the tea tray down on the table he knew at that moment she was someone he wanted to get to know better in the process.

"It's herbal tea. Do you want me to add any type of sweetener?" she asked.

"No," he said flatly, although he wasn't sure if he did or not. He wasn't a hot tea drinker, but did enjoy a glass of cold sweet tea from time to time. However, for some reason he felt he would probably enjoy his hot tea like he did his coffee—without anything added to it.

"I prefer mine sweet," she said softly, turning and smiling over at him. His guts tightened and he tried like hell to ignore the ache deep within and the attraction for this woman. He'd never felt anything like this before.

He was still standing and when she crossed the room toward him carrying his cup of tea, he had to forcibly propel air through his lungs with every step she took. Her beauty was brutal to the eyes but soothing to the soul, and he was enjoying the view in deep male appreciation. How old was she and what was she doing out here in the middle of nowhere trying to run a ranch?

"Here you are, Jason."

He liked the sound of his name from her lips and when he took the glass from her hands they touched in the process. Immediately, he felt his stomach muscles begin to clench.

king ventures. That was how he'd met her
vannah socialite, daughter of a shipping
ten years her senior. The marriage had
ore on increasing their wealth instead of
s well aware of both of her parents' sup-
eet affairs.

as Kenneth Bostwick was concerned, she
rman's widowed father at the age of sev-
a thirty-something-year-old woman and
een their only child. Bella gathered from
s she'd overheard from Kenneth's daugh-
Kenneth and Herman had never gotten
Herman thought Kenneth's mother, Be-
een anything but a gold digger who mar-
enough to be her grandfather.

it Herman had a granddaughter came as
veryone around these parts."

led softly. "Yes, and it came as quite a
to discover I had a grandfather."

e surprise that touched his face. "You
out Herman?"

ght both my father's parents were dead.
s close to forty when he married my
en I was in my teens he was in his fif-
I assumed his parents were deceased
mentioned them. I didn't know about
got a summons to be present at the read-
My parents didn't even mention anything
al. They attended the services but only
leaving town to take care of business. I
one of their usual business trips. It was
returned that they mentioned that Her-

"Thanks," he said, thinking he needed to step away from her and not let Bella Bostwick crowd his space. But he also very much wanted to keep her right there. Topping the list was her scent. He wasn't sure what perfume she was wearing but it was definitely an attention grabber, although her beauty alone would do the trick.

"You're welcome. Now I suggest we sit down or I'm going to get a crick in my neck staring up at you."

He heard the smile in her voice and then saw it on her lips. It stirred to life something inside of him and for a moment he wondered if her smile was genuine or practiced and quickly came to the conclusion it was genuine. During his thirty-four years he had met women who'd been as phony as a four-dollar bill but he had a feeling Bella Bostwick wasn't one of them. In fact, she might be a little too real for her own good.

"I don't want that to happen," he said, easing down on her sofa and stretching his long legs out in front of him. He watched as she then eased down in the comfortable-looking recliner he had bought Herman five years ago for his seventy-fifth birthday.

Jason figured this was probably one of the craziest things he'd ever done, sit with a woman in her living room in the middle of the day and converse with her while sipping tea. But he was doing it and at that moment, he couldn't imagine any other place he'd rather be.

Bella took a sip of her tea and studied Jason over the rim of her cup. Who was he? Why was she so attracted to him? And why was he attracted to her? And she knew the latter was true. She'd felt it that night at the ball and she could feel it now. He was able to bring out desires in her that she'd never felt before but for some reason she didn't feel threatened by those feelings. Instead, although she really didn't know him, she felt he was a powerhouse of strength, tenderness and protectiveness all rolled into one. She knew he would never hurt her.

"So, tell me about yourself, Jason," she heard herself say, wanting so much to hear about the man who seemed to be taking up so much space in her living room as well as in her mind.

A smile touched his lips when he said, "I'm a Westmoreland."

His words raised her curiosity up a notch. Was being a Westmoreland supposed to mean something? She hadn't heard any type of arrogance or egotism in his words, just a sense of pride, self-respect and honor.

"And what does being a Westmoreland mean?" she asked as she tucked her legs beneath her to get more comfortable in the chair.

She watched him take a sip of his tea. "There's a bunch of us, fifteen in fact," Jason said.

She nodded, taking in his response. "Fifteen?"

"Yes. And that's not counting the three Westmoreland wives and a cousin-in-law from Australia. In our family tree we've now become known as the Denver Westmorelands."

"Denver Westmorelands? Does that mean there are more Westmorelands in other parts of the country?"

"Yes, there are some who sprung from the Atlanta area. We have fifteen cousins there, as well. Most of them were at the Westmoreland charity ball."

An amused smile touched her lips. She recalled seeing them and remembered thinking how much they'd resembled in looks or height. Jason had been the only one she'd gotten a real good close-up view of, and the only

"Thanks," he said, thinking he needed to step away from her and not let Bella Bostwick crowd his space. But he also very much wanted to keep her right there. Topping the list was her scent. He wasn't sure what perfume she was wearing but it was definitely an attention grabber, although her beauty alone would do the trick.

"You're welcome. Now I suggest we sit down or I'm going to get a crick in my neck staring up at you."

He heard the smile in her voice and then saw it on her lips. It stirred to life something inside of him and for a moment he wondered if her smile was genuine or practiced and quickly came to the conclusion it was genuine. During his thirty-four years he had met women who'd been as phony as a four-dollar bill but he had a feeling Bella Bostwick wasn't one of them. In fact, she might be a little too real for her own good.

"I don't want that to happen," he said, easing down on her sofa and stretching his long legs out in front of him. He watched as she then eased down in the comfortable-looking recliner he had bought Herman five years ago for his seventy-fifth birthday.

Jason figured this was probably one of the craziest things he'd ever done, sit with a woman in her living room in the middle of the day and converse with her while sipping tea. But he was doing it and at that moment, he couldn't imagine any other place he'd rather be.

Bella took a sip of her tea and studied Jason over the rim of her cup. Who was he? Why was she so attracted to him? And why was he attracted to her? And she knew the latter was true. She'd felt it that night at the ball and she could feel it now. He was able to bring out desires in her that she'd never felt before but for some reason one she'd held a conversation with before her uncle had practically dragged her away from the party that night.

She then decided to bring up something she'd detected at the ball. "You and my uncle Kenneth don't get along."

If her statement surprised him the astonishment was not reflected in his face. "No, we've never gotten along," he said as if the thought didn't bother him, in fact he preferred it that way.

She paused and waited on him to elaborate but he didn't. He just took another sip of tea.

"And why is that?"

He shrugged massive shoulders and the gesture made her body even more responsive to his. "I can't rightly say why we've never seen eye-to-eye on a number of things."

"What about my grandfather? Did you get along with him?"

He chuckled. "Actually I did. Herman and I had a good relationship that started back when I was kid. He taught me a lot about ranching and I enjoyed our chats."

She took a sip of her tea. "Did he ever mention anything about having a granddaughter?"

"No, but then I didn't know he had a son, either. The only family I knew about was Kenneth and their relationship was rather strained."

She nodded. She'd heard the story of how her father had left for college at the age of seventeen, never to return. Her uncle Kenneth claimed he wasn't sure what the disagreement had been between the two men since he himself had been a young kid at the time. David Bostwick had made his riches on the East Coast, first as a land developer and then as an investor in all sorts of moneymaking ventures. That was how he'd met her mother, a Savannah socialite, daughter of a shipping magnate and ten years her senior. The marriage had been based more on increasing their wealth instead of love. She was well aware of both of her parents' supposedly discreet affairs.

And as far as Kenneth Bostwick was concerned, she knew that Herman's widowed father at the age of seventy married a thirty-something-year-old woman and Kenneth had been their only child. Bella gathered from bits and pieces she'd overheard from Kenneth's daughter, Elyse, that Kenneth and Herman had never gotten along because Herman thought Kenneth's mother, Belinda, hadn't been anything but a gold digger who married a man old enough to be her grandfather.

"Finding out Herman had a granddaughter came as a surprise to everyone around these parts."

Bella chuckled softly. "Yes, and it came as quite a surprise to me to discover I had a grandfather."

She saw the surprise that touched his face. "You didn't know about Herman?"

"No. I thought both my father's parents were dead. My father was close to forty when he married my mother and when I was in my teens he was in his fifties already so I assumed his parents were deceased since he never mentioned them. I didn't know about Herman until I got a summons to be present at the reading of the will. My parents didn't even mention anything about the funeral. They attended the services but only said they were leaving town to take care of business. I assumed it was one of their usual business trips. It was only when they returned that they mentioned that Her-